THE LITTLE
DRUMMER BOY

THE LITTLE

DRUMMER BOY

Ezra Jack Keats

Words and Music by Katherine Davis,
Henry Onorati and Harry Simeone

MACMILLAN PUBLISHING CO., INC.
New York
COLLIER MACMILLAN PUBLISHERS
London

Copyright © Ezra Jack Keats 1968. *The Little Drummer Boy* by H. Simeone, H. Onorati and K. Davis. Copyright © 1958 by Mills Music, Inc. and International Korwin Corp. Used by permission. All rights reserved. No part of this book may be reproduced or transmitted in any form or by any means, electronic or mechanical, including photocopying, recording or by any information storage and retrieval system, without permission in writing from the Publisher.

Macmillan Publishing Co., Inc., 866 Third Avenue, New York, N.Y.
Collier Macmillan Canada Ltd. Library of Congress catalog card number: 68-25714.
Printed in the United States of America. ISBN 0-02-749530-2   5 6 7 8 9 10

Come, they told me,
(pa-rum-pum-pum-pum)

Our newborn King to see,
(pa-rum-pum-pum-pum)

Our finest gifts to bring
(pa-rum-pum-pum-pum)

To lay before the King,
(pa-rum-pum-pum-pum, rum-pum-pum-pum, rum-pum-pum-pum)

So to honor Him
(*pa-rum-pum-pum-pum*)

When we come.

Baby Jesus,
(pa-rum-pum-pum-pum)

I am a poor boy too,

(pa-rum-pum-pum-pum)

I have no gift to bring
(*pa-rum-pum-pum-pum*)

That's fit to give a king,
(*pa-rum-pum-pum-pum,*
rum-pum-pum-pum,
rum-pum-pum-pum)

Shall I play for you
(pa-rum-pum-pum-pum)

On my drum?

Mary nodded,
(pa-rum-pum-pum-pum)

The ox and lamb kept time,
(pa-rum-pum-pum-pum)

I played my drum for Him,
(*pa-rum-pum-pum-pum*)

I played my best for Him,
(pa-rum-pum-pum-pum,
rum-pum-pum-pum,
rum-pum-pum-pum)

Then He smiled at me,
(*pa-rum-pum-pum-pum*)

Me and my drum.

The Little Drummer Boy

Words and Music by KATHERINE DAVIS, HENRY ONORATI and HARRY SIMEONE

MODERATO

Come, they told me, pa-rum pum pum pum — Our new-born

King to see, pa-rum pum pum pum — Our fin-est gifts to bring, pa-

rum pum pum pum — To lay be - fore the King, pa- rum pum pum pum,

rum pum pum pum, rum pum pum pum — So to hon- or Him, pa-

rum pum pum pum — When — we come. —

August

K. C. KELLEY • BOB OSTROM

The Child's World

Published by The Child's World®
1980 Lookout Drive • Mankato, MN 56003-1705
800-599-READ • www.childsworld.com

Acknowledgments
The Child's World®: Mary Berendes, Publishing Director
The Design Lab: Design
Jody Jensen Shaffer: Editing and Fact-Checking

Photo credits
© Georgios Kollidas/Shutterstock.com: 22 (bottom);
gosphotodesign/Shutterstock.com: 10; Jose Gil/Dreamstime.
com: 23 (top); Kochneva Tetyana/Shutterstock.com: 12 (top);
Library of Congress: 20 (bottom); magnez2/iStock.com: 19
(top); meunierd/Shutterstock.com: 19 (bottom); Michael Dechev/
Shutterstock.com: 13 (Bottom); Michael Pettigrew/Shutterstock.com:
13 (top); monkeybusinessimages/iStock.com: 12 (bottom); spirit of
america/Shutterstock.com: 22 (top); Susan S. Carroll/Shutterstock.
com: 6; Tilo G/Shutterstock.com: 11 (bottom); TravnikovStudio/
Shutterstock.com: cover, 1, 5; USMC: 18; Warren Goldswain/
Shutterstock.com: 20 (top); Yourthstock/Shutterstock.com: 11 (top);
Zatletic/Dreamstime.com: 23 (bottom)

ISBN 9781626873636
LCCN 2014930702

Printed in the United States of America
Mankato, MN
July, 2014
PA02214

ABOUT THE AUTHOR

K.C. Kelley has written dozens of books for young readers on everything from sports to nature to history. He was born in January, loves April because that's when baseball begins, and loves to take vacations in August!

ABOUT THE ILLUSTRATOR

Bob Ostrom has been illustrating books for twenty years. A graduate of the New England School of Art & Design at Suffolk University, Bob has worked for such companies as Disney, Nickelodeon, and Cartoon Network. He lives in North Carolina with his wife and three children.

Contents

WELCOME TO AUGUST!

Hot enough for you? August is usually the hottest month in most of the United States and Canada. It's a great month to head to the beach or to the woods to cool off! August is also the only month without a big, national holiday.

August

Order: Eighth

Days: 31

LITTLE LEAGUE

In August, millions of people tune in to watch the Little League World Series. The top U.S. teams face teams from around the world. Teams of 11- and 12-year-olds battle for the big prize! The games are only one part of the fun. For the players, the best part is meeting kids from other nations.

HOW DID AUGUST GET ITS NAME?

The ancient Romans named this month for Augustus Caesar, a famous leader. This month used to have 30 days. The Romans wanted Augustus to have 31 like July, named for Julius Caesar. So they took a day from February. That's why August has 31 days!

Birthstone

Each month has a stone linked to it. People who have birthdays in that month call it their birthstone. For August, it's the peridot.

AUGUST AROUND THE WORLD

Here is the name of this month
in other languages.

Chinese	Bā yuè
Dutch	Augustus
English	August
French	Août
German	der August
Italian	Agosto
Japanese	Hachigatsu
Spanish	Agosto
Swahili	Agosti

THANKS, JAMES!

On August 10, 1846, "America's Attic" was established. That's the nickname of the Smithsonian Institution. That famous museum began thanks to a British man named James Smithson. For an unknown reason, Smithson gave $500,000 to the United States to open a museum. Since then, the Smithsonian has grown to include more than 18 other museums in and around Washington D.C.

BIG AUGUST HOLIDAYS

Left-handers' Day, August 13

On August 13, Americans enjoy Left-handers' Day! Here are some of the most famous people who were left-handed:

Neil Armstrong: astronaut
Bill Clinton: former U.S. President
Marie Curie: physicist, chemist, and Nobel Prize winner
Leonardo da Vinci: artist and inventor
Albert Einstein: physicist
Gerald Ford: former U.S. President
Bill Gates: businessman, inventor, and philanthropist
John McEnroe: tennis champion
Barack Obama: U.S. President
Julia Roberts: actress
Babe Ruth: baseball hero
Ringo Starr: drummer
Oprah Winfrey: TV host, actress, and producer

National Aviation Day, August 19

Today is the day to honor the people who invented airplanes, as well as other flying heroes. Brothers Orville and Wilbur Wright made the first airplane flight in December 1903. They were the first to figure out the right shape for wings. Their engine powered them into the sky. And they created the ways that airplanes are steered.

WHY AUGUST 19?

Why August 19? That was Orville Wright's birthday! Wilbur and Orville got their start making bicycles in Ohio. They were inspired by other inventors to look at flying. They flew for the first time on a sand dune in Kitty Hawk, North Carolina. A monument there marks their feat.

FUN AUGUST DAYS

August has more ways to celebrate than just cooling off in the shade! Here are some of the unusual holidays you can enjoy in August:

First Saturday

National Mustard Day

August 3

National Watermelon Day

August 6

Wiggle-Your-Toes Day

August 7

National Lighthouse Day

August 13

Left-Handers' Day

August 20

National Radio Day

August 21

Senior Citizens' Day

12

August 26

National Dog Day

August 30

Toasted Marshmallow Day

August 31

National Trail Mix Day

AUGUST WEEKS AND MONTHS

Holidays don't just mean days…you can celebrate for a week, too! You can also have fun all month long. Find out more about these ways to enjoy August!

AUGUST WEEKS

International Clown Week: If you have a goofy wig and a clown nose, wear it—it's time to celebrate clowns! Clowning is a big part of circus life. Clowns have to be great jugglers and acrobats, too.

International Assistance Dog Week: Thousands of dogs are trained to help people. These animals guide blind people. They help disabled kids and adults. They can even help feed people!

AUGUST MONTHS

National Golf Month: Did you know golf has been around for more than 600 years? Shepherds in Scotland started the game. They hit rocks with their shepherd staffs! Today, millions around the world love this sport. In August, tee it up to celebrate!

National Peach Month: Juicy, sweet, tasty: peaches are one of our favorite fruits. This month, the peach harvest is winding down. Make sure and get some fresh peaches before they disappear!

National Picnic Month: What's more pleasant than a picnic? This month, gather your family and eat outdoors. You can have a picnic in the park, at the beach, or even in your backyard! (Watch out for ants!)

AUGUST AROUND THE WORLD

Countries around the world celebrate in August. Find these countries on the map. Then read about how people there have fun in August!

August 1

Swiss National Day, Switzerland
Switzerland became the first **republic** in 1291. A republic is a government in which people get to vote for leaders.

INTERNATIONAL YOUTH DAY

August 12 is International Youth Day. The **United Nations** wants people to know more about kids. The annual Youth Day spreads news about kids. In 2013, for example, the day was about children who have to leave their homelands. In other years, the focus was on **poverty** or disease. Kids are the future. We have to take care of them!

August 20

St. Stephens Day, Hungary
Hungary became one nation more than one thousand years ago. St. Stephen was the first king. The nation celebrates on this day with parades, concerts, and more.

August 15

State Holiday, Liechtenstein
One of Europe's smallest countries celebrates today. Most of its people gather at the prince's castle in Vaduz. A daylong party ends with fireworks!

AUGUST IN HISTORY

August 3, 1492

Christopher Columbus left Spain on his journey to find another sea route to Asia.

August 6, 1926

American swimmer Gertrude Ederle became the first women to swim across the English Channel.

A DREAM SPEECH

On August 28, 1963, Martin Luther King, Jr. spoke in Washington D.C. A huge crowd had gathered for a **civil rights** march. King's speech is one of the most famous in American history. "I have a dream today," he said. He called on people to unite no matter what their color. His dream was to have a nation and a world where people lived together in peace. Do you think his dream has come true yet? How are you helping to make that dream become real?

August 8, 1974

Richard Nixon **resigned** from being president. That means he left office on his own. He was the first president to do so.

August 1–9, 1936

American track star Jesse Owens won four gold medals at the Berlin Olympics.

August 14, 1945

World War II in the Pacific ended when Japan surrendered.

August 15, 1914

The Panama Canal opened. For the first time, ships could sail between the Atlantic and Pacific without going around South America.

August 27, 1883

A volcano erupted on an island called Krakatoa. It was near Java. It was one of the biggest explosions ever. The noise could be heard 3,000 miles away!

August 30, 1967

Thurgood Marshall joined the U.S. Supreme Court. He was the first African-American to earn that important job.

NEW STATES!

Three states first joined the United States in August. Do you live in any of these? If you do, then make sure and say, "Happy Birthday!" to your state.

Colorado
August 1, 1876

Missouri
August 10, 1821

Hawai`i
August 21, 1959

FAMOUS AUGUST BIRTHDAYS

August 3

Tom Brady
This great quarterback has won three Super Bowls.

August 15

Napoleon Bonaparte
The emperor of France was once Europe's most powerful leader.

August 18

Virginia Dare
In 1587, she became the first English child born in what is now the United States.

August 19

Bill Clinton

He was President of the United States from 1993–2001.

August 23

Kobe Bryant

This basketball star has won five NBA titles.

August 26

Mother Teresa

This Catholic nun helped thousands of sick people in India and inspired millions of people with her work.

HAPPY BIRTHDAY, MR. PRESIDENT!

Barack Obama was born August 4, 1961, in Hawai`i. He grew up and went to high school there. For a while, he lived in Indonesia, too. Obama went to Harvard University. While he was a senator from Illinois, he ran for president. He was first elected in 2008 and re-elected in 2012. Obama was the first African-American to be chosen for president.

GLOSSARY

civil rights (SIV-ul RYTS) The rights all people have to freedom and equal treatment.

poverty (POV-ur-tee) The state of being very poor.

republic (ree-PUB-lik) A government where the people choose their leaders.

resigned (ree-ZYND) Gave up a job.

United Nations (yoo-NY-ted NAY-shunz) An organization of nations that works together to solve problems and strives for peace.

INDEX